Richard L Henry

The Late Michael Henry

Richard L Henry

The Late Michael Henry

ISBN/EAN: 9783744717670

Printed in Europe, USA, Canada, Australia, Japan

Cover: Foto ©Raphael Reischuk / pixelio.de

More available books at **www.hansebooks.com**

THE LATE

MICHAEL HENRY.

OBITUARY NOTICES,

LETTERS OF CONDOLENCE,

AND OTHER MEMENTOES.

PRINTED FOR PRIVATE CIRCULATION.

LONDON:

PRINTED BY J. M. JOHNSON & SONS, LIMITED,

56, HATTON GARDEN.

1875.

TO

LIONEL VAN OVEN,

THE OLDEST AND MOST VALUED

FRIEND OF

THE LATE MICHAEL HENRY,

THIS SHORT SERIES OF

OBITUARY NOTICES,

LETTERS OF CONDOLENCE,

AND OTHER MEMENTOES,

COLLECTED AND COMPILED BY HIS AFFECTIONATE BROTHER,

RICHARD L. HENRY,

IS

DEDICATED,

WITH THE WARMEST FEELINGS OF

FRIENDSHIP AND REGARD.

My dear Lionel,

To you, as the oldest and most valued Friend of my late and much lamented Brother, Michael Henry, I dedicate this Collection of Letters of Condolence sent to his Family, and Biographical Notices written on the occasion of his most unfortunate and sudden death.

I never knew until too late how much he was appreciated by the Jewish Community, nor until a short time before his death was I at all aware how hard he laboured in all social and religious matters, for the benefit and improvement of our co-religionists.

Circumstances known only to you and two or three others brought my lamented and much beloved brother and myself very closely in contact with each other during the last few months of his life, and it was not until then that I became aware of his

total abnegation of Self, and his devoted-
ness to the interests of our Community.

It is the knowledge that I now have of
the nature of his labours that has induced
me to collect these gratifying memorials in
recognition of his merits, and it is your
very intimate acquaintance with his feelings
and his character that has been another
reason why I should dedicate this collection
to you.

My impression with these ideas must be
my apology for addressing you without your
knowledge upon a subject that is so deeply
engraven on my heart, and I am sure you
will appreciate this trifling tribute to his
memory.

Believe me,

My dear Lionel,

Faithfully yours,

RICHARD L. HENRY.

To Lionel Van Oven, Esq.

OBITUARY NOTICES.

"JEWISH CHRONICLE," JUNE 18, 1875.

DEATH OF MR. MICHAEL HENRY.

BOWED down grief-stricken and with a trembling hand, we trace these lines. Alas! the blow is so heavy, so sudden, that our fingers almost refuse us their services.

Last evening (we write this on Wednesday night) the popular, amiable, most kind-hearted and truly religious Editor of this paper—Michael Henry—full of hope and high and noble aspirations, still moved cheerfully in the land of the living; and this evening—we can hardly realize it to ourselves—his body lies on the ground stiff and cold—a corpse. The news of his dissolution quickly followed that of the sad accident which had befallen him. His clothes accidently caught fire, and he succumbed to the terrible shock which his delicate nervous system thereby sustained. He closed his earthly career

in the prime of life—at the age of forty-five—precisely
at the period when his fine mental powers were at their
zenith; when the performances of the past held out
bright promises of still greater achievements in the
future.

All that have seen this genial face beaming with
benevolence, and this high forehead the seat of a chaste,
almost feminine imagination, and a manly, vigourous
intellect, will carry with them the images thereof through
life. And well does he deserve to be remembered; for
in his bosom beat a truly Jewish philanthropic heart,
profoundly sympathising with all that was great and
good. It was the seat of a soul almost virginal in its
purity, transparent like the crystal.

It is not our intention this week to write his obituary.
If we would, we could not. At this moment we cannot
think. We can only feel—feel for ourselves, feel for the
bereaved family, feel for the community to which he
clung with every fibre of a heart overflowing with affection, and to which he had endeared himself by extra-
ordinary devotion to its cause, and by rare services
rendered to it. At this moment we can only mourn,
mourn, mourn, over the woful loss sustained by all of us!
Next week, no doubt, more competent hands and loving
hearts will undertake the sad task of doing justice to the
memory of this much beloved and much respected
righteous man.

Ascend then to Heaven thou pure spirit! Thou wast too good for this sinful world! Go receive thy reward at the hands of thy Maker whom thou so faithfully servedst from childhood. Thine the gain, ours the loss. Thine the bliss of eternity, ours the grief in our span of life.

יקר בעיני ה׳ המותה לחסידיו׳

"JEWISH WORLD," JUNE 18, 1875.

The whole community will learn with profound sorrow of the demise of Mr. Michael Henry, who for some years, and up to the time of his death, edited our contemporary the *Jewish Chronicle.* On Tuesday evening, while at his office in Fleet Street, his attire accidently became ignited by fire; and although every effort was exerted to stay the progress of the flames, it was found that he had sustained most fearful injuries. He was removed to his private residence in Argyll Square, where, after lingering about twenty-four hours, he succumbed to his terrible agonies on Wednesday evening.

The limited time at our disposal precludes us from giving more than the briefest details touching the melancholy event. The great esteem in which deceased was universally held by every individual with whom he came into contact, either in his private or professional capacity, is a matter generally known, and his untimely death will cast a gloom in all circles of the Anglo-Jewish community.

Mr. Henry had not yet attained his 45th year.

It is expected that the funeral will take place on Sunday next.

"NORTH BRITISH ADVERTISER AND JOURNAL."

TO THE EDITOR.

Some years ago you inserted a notice of the death of the mother of this distinguished man, whose untimely loss to the Jewish community has been deplored by the Jewish press and the Jewish preachers in London—the scene of his busy and useful life. A Scotch Editor and Presbyterian, familiar with his writings, pays the impartial tribute to his memory which I subjoin. Mr. M. Henry, though a "Hebrew of the Hebrews," was a patriotic Englishman and a friend of the whole human race. He combined in himself the genius and moral qualities which go to constitute the clever *littérateur*, the candid controversialist, the man of business, the untiring but retiring philanthropist, the faithful friend, the loving son, and affectionate brother. I have often regretted that those great qualities which still distinguish the illustrious race from which he sprang, and of which he was so justly proud, are so little known and appreciated in the northern part of the island. The south has abandoned much of her ancient prejudices, for instead of being governed by members of great historical families, she now consents to be ruled by one in whose veins flow only Jewish blood, and who has reached his proud position by his own unaided but commanding genius. P. S.

LETTER FROM A SCOTCH EDITOR.

" Formerly a journalist in one of the large towns of England, where there was a numerous Jewish community, the *Jewish Chronicle* came constantly under my notice for several years. I was particularly struck with the character of the editorial articles in it. They invariably exhibited a remarkable breadth of human sympathy in combination with an unusually clear and vigorous understanding. I was not then aware that the writer was the late Michael Henry, whose melancholy death not only deprives his co-religionists of one of the brightest ornaments of their faith, but one of the most serious losses I have ever known to the denominational literature of this country. Deeply religious, he was yet one of those rare men who soar above creeds, embracing all goodness in their sweep. Men who are, as it were, the property of the whole world, and whose candour, justice, and impartiality are respected and admired when their conclusions are very often rejected."

"JEWISH CHRONICLE," JUNE 25, 1875.

When some days ago it became our melancholy duty to announce the death of the much lamented Michael Henry, we had only strength to utter a cry of anguish. A week has since elapsed. The dead has been buried out of sight, earth returned to earth. We have in the interval been enabled to realise to ourselves the woful loss sustained. The stunning effect of the blow is wearing off, and the power of reflection gradually coming back, and we ask ourselves : What is the hidden spring of this general mourning, of this bitter grief, which so profoundly agitates the mind of the whole Anglo-Jewish community ? This community has unfortunately sustained before severe losses by the death of still younger men of uncommon promise and considerable performance. There was the late Barnett Abrahams cut off in the prime of life in the midst of a most useful and benevolent career ; and if not as suddenly, still more prematurely. There was the late Numa Hartog, a fragrant blossom nipped before even the bud was formed. Great was the sympathy exhibited on those occasions. Nevertheless it must be admitted it equalled neither in depth nor in breadth that just now so powerfully stirring up the soul of the metropolitan Jewish community.

What, we ask again, was the hidden spring of this

profound and universal emotion? It was not fas-
cinating or imposing personal appearance. It was not
rank or wealth, for the deceased was not a scion of any
of those leading families to whom the mere accident of
birth already secures a certain social position, nor was
he born, as the proverb has it, with a silver spoon in his
mouth. He was essentially a self-made man. He shone
neither by a towering genius nor commanding elo-
quence which often carry away, and in one single
moment achieve triumphs which talent, vigour of intellect, and an unspotted integrity not rarely fail to
accomplish in the course of a long and laborious life.

The secret which gave the deceased this power over
our emotional side we unhesitatingly say was his profoundly sympathetic nature, and the genuine kind-
heartedness reflected not only by an uncommonly
benevolent countenance, but by every word he uttered,
every gesture which accompanied it, and every act he
performed. It was not less the act itself than the mode
in which it was performed. The sincere joy which
lighted up his face when he could serve, giving to a
favour shown the appearance of one received, as well
as the regret depicted on his whole being when he could
not render the service solicited, were equally characteristic of the goodness of his heart, and consequently
whether granting or refusing equally gained him the
regard of those concerned. He was much beloved

because he loved much.   His soul resembled a limpid
pool ; you could see down to its very depth and perceive
every emotion as it flitted across or settled down in a
permanent form.   His was a magnetic soul which
sympathetically drew to itself everything that was good
and noble.   You could not but admire a capacity to
work and a willingness to serve, such as only mark minds
of a superior order.   You could not but love a simplicity
so childlike that it was all but incapable to suspect
guile ; and you could not but respect a character as
firm in its grasp of what was just and good, as per-
severing and undaunted in the execution of its behests
however arduous the task.   He exercised an irresistible
charm over the minds of all those with whom he came
into contact, evoked and roused their better self from
the depth in which it happened to slumber, simply because they instinctively felt that they had before them
one of those unsophisticated genuine natures—Heaven's
choicest and noblest works—which loved goodness for
goodness sake, and over which the seductive attractions
of evanescent gratification, so irresistible to the gene-
rality of mankind, had lost their power.

If hypocrisy be the homage which vice renders to
virtue, what must be the tribute which the genuine sentiment pays to it ?   And who that has witnessed the
profound general sorrow, that has listened to the touching expression given it from the pulpit, at public meet-

ings, and indeed at every gathering, whether of a public
or private character, that has seen the large grave funeral
procession as it wound along, the sad faces and tear-
dimmed eyes of the beloved charges of the deceased—
the boys of the Stepney School—heard the quivering
tremulous voice of the officiating minister, and the loud
sobs as the cold clods of earth rolled over the coffin in
the grave,—who, we say, witnessing and hearing all this,
could have doubted the genuineness and depth of the
feeling which the melancholy event stirred up in every
heart ☙

But while indulging in this just grief, let us not neg-
lect to derive such lessons from the bereavement as its
consideration is capable of yielding. It is, in the first
place, another exemplification of the superiority of heart
over head, of sentiment over intellect. "One touch of
nature makes the whole world kin." What hero, what
genius could have received such tribute of sympathy as
was paid at this grave? It, in the second place, fur-
nishes a gratifying proof that, however materialistic the
age, and however prevalent utilitarian views, idealism is
not quite extinct, at least not in the Jewish community,
and the capability of appreciating pure spiritual worth
has happily not yet been obliterated amongst us; since
no consideration which mere earthly distinction is able
to confer could have called forth the voluntary tokens
of love and marks of respect bestowed upon the remains

of this humble, unpretending pilgrim at the premature close of his career.

And while acknowledging the rare worth of the departed, the beneficent effect of his activity in the community, while endeavouring to fix for life his beloved image in our souls, shall nothing be done to perpetuate his memory amongst us? Shall his memory, like a meteor illuming the sky for a moment, be allowed to sink for ever in the night of oblivion? Shall nothing testify to our children this bright passage over our communal horizon? There are those among our leading men who have known how to appreciate his worth. There are those who were associated with him in his labours and shared his aspirations. Let them but speak the word, and all classes of the community will cheerfully rally round them. Give but the signal, and a monument will rise to his memory, such as he would have approved could he but have been consulted; such as would show that we were worthy of him; such as would link the present to the future—such as would encourage our children to emulate the model presented to them in the days of their fathers.

"JEWISH CHRONICLE," JUNE 25, 1875.

The following sketch of the life of the late lamented Michael Henry has been forwarded to us. It is the composition of one who was from childhood intimately associated with the deceased, and who had early in life learned to appreciate his worth, to admire his talents and love his virtues.

Michael Henry was born at Kennington, on the 19th of February, 1830. His father was a merchant; his mother a lady of more than ordinary attainments, well read and highly educated. He had scarcely completed his third year when the family (of whom he was the youngest) removed to Ramsgate, on account of his father's declining health.

At a very early age he showed evidence of genius and poetical imagination far beyond his years, and it was deemed necessary to prevent him from pursuing any studies, lest he should overtax his strength. He however managed to acquire a larger amount of knowledge than most of his companions, and when about six years old, used to astonish visitors at the house by the extent and variety of his information, his favourite plaything was a terrestial globe, and his favourite amusement to write scraps of poetry which, even at that early age, he did with amazing facility. When eight years old he was sent to a school at Ramsgate, where he made great progress, and where he remained for two years. Immediately after his father's death in April, 1840, the family came to London, and his education then began at the City of London School, at which he was a scholar for four years.

In June, 1844, he left school, and was sent to a sister then residing in Paris, where a situation in a counting house had been offered to him ; but it soon became evident that he could not content himself with the ordinary routine of a commercial office ; and as the limited means at his mother's disposal necessitated his contributing something towards his own support, he accepted with pleasure an offer to enter the office of the late James Robertson, Patent Agent, and Editor of the *Mechanics' Magazine.*

In the semi-scientific and literary employment there he took great pleasure, and whilst he remained in that situation he assisted mainly in the Editor's department. Some time after the death of Mr. Robertson he resolved to establish a business as Patent Agent on his own account, which he commenced in 1857, and carried on up to the period of his death.

In the course of time he began to assist Dr. Benisch in his editorial labours in connection with this journal, and upon the retirement of that gentleman in 1868, became its editor. By the manner in which he filled that difficult and responsible post, he won the esteem and regard not only of his coadjutors, but of the Jewish public generally. Such is a brief outline of his life, and it is a tale easily told. It is far more difficult to convey to our readers an adequate idea of his unselfish character and of his many noble and praiseworthy acts.

His mind was essentially poetic and his earnest faith in the principles of Judaism was remarkable. From his earliest years he not only wrote poetry with ease, but when a lad of nine years old he composed prayers for his own use on various occasions. In 1836 (when he was six years old) there was a fearful storm at Ramsgate, and he saw a shipwreck from the windows of the house. He was terrified at the occurrence and wrote as follows :—

> " No more, no more the sea is calm,
> The ships now sound a deaf alarm,
> .The barques do roll in every form,
> Such is the raging of the storm ;
> Oh God ! I offer prayers to Thee,
> To stop the raging of the sea."

In 1843 (when 13 years of age) he visited some friends at Boulogne, and wrote there a short novel dealing humorously with the incidents which occur to English travellers abroad ; the reading of this from day to day amused the whole party, and some of the ideas and characteristic sketches still retain their hold on the memory of those who survive. His writings of this class and other humorous sketches would fill volumes, and few who read his later productions could imagine that in his youth he possessed such a fund of genuine humour and sharp satire. His love of charity was so great, that when quite a child he desired to found a charity, and put aside a portion of his pocket money for that purpose. At length this wish assumed a practical shape, and he founded in

1847 the General Benevolent Association, of which he has been ever since the Honorary Secretary. He was for a long time a member of the Council of Jews' College and of the Board of Deputies, and sat on the committees of other educational charities, which he aided by his personal supervision. But chief of all to him was the Stepney Jewish Schools. He not only acted as Honorary Secretary to the Committee, but he devoted much of his valuable time (spare time, he had none) to the personal supervision of the boys in that school. He encouraged them by gifts, treats and prizes, he exhorted them to be good, truthful and industrious, and he lived to see some of them realize his hopes. He regarded them as objects of his loving care, and they have frequently evinced their appreciation of his affectionate solicitude.

Among his labours mention should be made of his constant aid to the Society for Diffusion of Religious Knowledge. As writer, lecturer, and promoter, he greatly assisted the Association in its earlier days, and fostered and aided many of the movements which arose from it, in extension of the original plan, such as the Sunday Evening Lectures and the Jewish Working Men's Club. He also originated the idea of a Life Boat Fund from the savings of school boys, and bestowed great attention on the scheme which some boys started at his suggestion.

His love for boys generally, and his desire to evince that love, was a remarkable feature in his character. He was never happier than when examining a class, delivering a lecture at a school, or distributing prizes, and to many of such distributions he contributed a prize himself. In the profession to which he belonged he was generally esteemed and respected, and on some important occasions his opinion was eagerly sought and highly valued, especially on questions of Patent Law, upon which he wrote a pamphlet, which was highly considered by the Committee of the House of Commons appointed to report on that subject. He was an Associate of the Society of Civil Engineers, and a member of other learned bodies. It was, however, as Editor of this journal that he was best known; and none but those who worked with him can fully appreciate his energetic labours to promote the welfare of the Jewish community, and to maintain peace and goodwill between the members of its various classes. Consistently attached to the principles and doctrines of his religion and its traditions, he was still tolerant towards those whose opinions differed from his own; and in many cases was enabled by his judicious management to pour oil on the troubled waters of rising disputes. It is almost superfluous to record in this journal that he was a pleasing and fluent writer, possessed of a poetic imagination, and that his language was both forcible and elegant. In private life he attracted the sincere friendship of a large circle of frends, both Jewish and Christian, of all grades and classes of society. His genial manners and pleasant conversation will be remembered long and often by many who now weep for his sudden and unlooked for death.

He died on Wednesday, the 16th inst., from the shock which his system received on his clothes taking fire rather than from the severity of the burns. The exact manner in which the melancholy accident occurred remains a mystery. But it appears that his shirt became ignited by the flame of a candle; and it is most probable that he threw off his outer clothes in the hope of disengaging himself from the burning garment, thus allowing the flames to obtain a mastery against which he could not contend. When assistance came it was found that he was much injured, but hopes of recovery were entertained. Unfortunately these hopes were not fulfilled, and he died in twenty-four hours. He was never married; but he had taken under his protection a sister and her three children, who, with the rest of his numerous family and countless friends, mourn for him with more than ordinary grief.

His funeral, which took place on Monday last, was attended by all the members of his family, and the procession which followed the hearse from the house consisted of nearly one hundred gentlemen, among whom were both the Chief Rabbis, almost all the Jewish clergy, and representatives of almost every grade and class of society and of several public Jewish institutions.

At the cemetery at Willesden a large concourse of people were assembled to meet the funeral. Boys from the Jews' Hospital, Deaf and Dumb Home, Gates of Hope School and Stepney Jewish Schools attended the funeral ; twelve of the latter carried the bier to the grave and were greatly affected. Almost every eye was dimmed with tears ; the coffin was covered with flowers which kind and sympathising friends had sent ; and the lowering of the body into its last resting place concluded one of the most impressive and solemn ceremonies that was ever witnessed. What deepened still more the solemnity was the circumstance that one of the deaf mute boys said the *Kaddish*. It was an ovation to *worth* such as no *wealth* could purchase; it was a display of feeling which our community may well be proud of— an evidence that the Jews of London can honour, respect, value and love those whose lives have deserved such a tribute. No monarch, no hero, no martyr was ever carried to his grave with greater honour, greater solemnity, greater respect and greater grief than Michael Henry.

A few of his friends contemplate a memorial, which will enable all who loved and respected him to give tangible expressions to their feelings. We are sure these friends will not appeal in vain.

"JEWISH CHRONICLE," JUNE 25, 1875.

On Sabbath last at several of the metropolitan synagogues the reverend preachers alluded to the death of Mr. Henry.

At the Central Synagogue the Rev. A. L. Green preached a sermon from the text: "That they may proclaim My name throughout all the earth." (Eccl. lx. 16). After commenting generally upon the text, and explaining the meaning of those phrases which, he said, are so familiar in the mouths of many, but are so strangely misunderstood, distorted and exaggerated, not only by the unreflective, but by the intelligent—viz., קדוש השם and חלול השם—the Sanctification of God and the profanation of His Holy Name, Mr. Green paused, and, in deep emotion, which was exhibited by every worshipper, he drew a pathetic picture of the life of one who was endeared to every member of the synagogue, and, indeed, as he was beloved by all who knew the singular amiability of his gentle nature. In broken voice, the Rev. Mr. Green showed how Michael Henry had devoted his life, לקדוש השם for the glorification of our holy faith. How every impulse was directed to improve and consolidate Judaic observances. How he eagerly seized every opportunity to throw his emotional nature into every measure having for its object the glory of God and the integrity of our common faith; and with what purity and nobility of purpose this, the main pursuit of his whole public life, had been effected. The united wealth of the world, said the preacher, could not, in his opinion, an opinion based on the friendship of years, have purchased or biassed his views. . The unselfishness of his life in this respect was well worthy of imitation by all, and it must and should be the desire on the part of the community to show its appreciation of such a career, interrupted by so untimely and lamentable an end, by associating the name of Michael Henry with some endearing communal memorial, which would doubtless be suggested by those whose practical wisdom should be our guide. The words of the preacher seemed to find a ready echo and a tearful response. All seemed to feel that while the community had lost a faithful and devoted friend ; while Judaism had lost an earnest advocate ; each worshipper had at the same time lost a personal and an affectionate friend.

The Rev. Dr. Hermann Adler commenced his discourse at Bayswater Synagogue on Sabbath last by saying that he had to choose one of two alternatives that day, either to be silent altogether, or else to speak of the terrible loss the community had sustained, for it was beyond his power to preach an ordinary sermon. He could not turn his pulpit teaching into hollow declamation, he could only speak of that of which his own heart and his hearers' hearts were full. He took his text from Isaiah lvii. 1, 2, and said: "We are now bewailing the loss of one whose sun has gone down while yet it was day, one who consecrated his life to the service of his people, who diffused a hallowed influence around him. Alas! How ill can the community spare such men as he! The memory of his goodness and worth is deathless and imperishable. His unselfish acts and noble words are written in the memory of the community, to whom, in truth, 'he clung with every fibre of his heart,' whom he served with rare conscientiousness and ability, and who will not suffer his name to perish in oblivion: who will not allow the good work he upheld in his life to languish. Have we then a right to deplore Michael Henry's death as early and premature? Can long life be measured by the arithmetic of months and years? God measures life by deeds, not by periods; not by decades or jubilees, but by glowing words, and actions that do not belie the speaker's words. Character, piety, activity is life, not years. To paraphase the well-known Talmudical adage, Michael Henry accomplished in his forty-four years more than another performs in a century. Now is not yet the time in which to recount all that our beloved brother was, all that he did. One fitting tribute I may pay his dear memory, by bidding him speak to the hearts of the two lads who have this day become Barmitzvah, for all the best traits of his character, his genial sympathy, his noble unselfishness, his all-absorbing love of Judaism came into prominence when he wrote of boys, or when he spoke to them. Thus he writes in a paper addressed to boys in the Sabbath Readings: ' Boys, you are the hope of the world! You are the heirs of the future, if time shall endure. When we who are writing for you, who think of you, and work for you, shall have passed away from this busy life, and shall be cold in our silent graves, you, if you are spared, will inherit our labours and our cares, and the world which we shall have left. . . . . . There is one recompense we all can understand, receive, and welcome. The young and the old, the happy and the sorrowful, the merry and the weary—we can all alike lift our eyes from earth, and hope to win the love of the Father in Heaven. May that light of love shine on you, boys, in the spring of your youth, and the summer of your manhood, in the autumn of declining strength and the winter of old age. Come boys of our hopes and affections; strive to be brave, wise and good, so that you may become better men than we are, so that your own boys in far days to come may profit by your exam-ple, and become better than you; and thus from gene-ration to generation improving and yet improving, while time and the world endure. . . . And when for us the silver cord is loosed for ever, keep our memory green and think of us tenderly, lovingly, and prayerfully.' " The congregation was deeply affected during the sermon.

The Rev. A. Löwy preached last Sabbath at the West London Synagogue (Berkeley Street). He took his text from Numbers ii. 2, which he translated thus: "Let every man stand by his banner which is marked with the ensigns of the paternal house : thus shall the Children of Israel be encamped, over against and round about the Tabernacle shall they be encamped." The sermon was chiefly historical and referred to various data in the Midrash. In the course of the sermon the preacher took occasion to advert to the uncertainties of life, especially as to the hour when man may be called away from the scenes of busy activity. Without mentioning by name him for whom the Jewish community now mourns, the friends of the departed were reminded of the great void occasioned by the untimely death of a loved and loving friend of his people. The rev. preacher observed: when a soul pure as silver leaves its earthly abode, "the Perpetual Light" in the synagogue recalls to the mind and to the heart the idea that the child of God shall emerge from darkness into light and combine strict attachment to the ancestral family with unswerving fidelity to the ancestral religion.

At the Borough Synagogue, the Rev. S. Singer took his text from that portion of the Sedrah of the day which records the conversation between Moses and Hobab relative to the intended departure of the latter for his native land—a step from which Moses endeavoured to dissuade him by pleading : " Forsake us not, we beseech thee, for thou knowest our encampment in the wilderness, and thou canst be to us in the place of eyes." The object of the discourse was to show how often human agencies and human means are employed to further the plans of Heaven. Towards the conclusion of his address the preacher spoke as follows : "To these reflections I have been more particularly led by a heavy calamity, with which the community has within the last few days been afflicted, through the sudden and mournful departure from our midst of one who also knew our encampment in the wilderness and was to us in the place of eyes. None could sympathize more fully than he with all the wants of his people ; none more deeply feel for all their sorrows and trials ; no one could join more heartily in all their joys and triumphs ; no one be more strongly imbued with their highest and most sacred hopes. To this power of sympathising with others he united the rarer power of working for others. His great and conspicuous talents were ever at the service of those who, in whatever form, sought the good of their people. His pen was 'the pen of a ready writer'—a pen wielded for many years with well sustained grace, energy and force of purpose, setting itself as its great aim the advancement of Israel and their elevation in the eyes of the nations of the earth. Yet was he who spared him-self so little ever considerate and generous towards the faults of others. If he was to us in the place of eyes, it was mainly to detect whatever good there was in the community. This gentle friend of ours, this friend of Israel's, filled a useful and important place. 'Despise not everybody, condemn not everything,' said the sage, 'for every man hath his hour and everything hath its place.' This principle appeared to have taken a firm hold of him. In every line of his writings one might trace that one idea, which is the truest expression of Jewish charity—there is some good in every thing, there is some merit in every body. But while all classes of the community found room in his affections, there was one section of it in particular to whose interests he seemed to address himself with an almost undivided ardour and devotion. He had, like many good men, an inextinguishable faith in youth; he had that mark of true manliness, a manly love for those who would themselves one day be men. It was with our lamented friend a rooted article of faith that in the young there was the germ, which waited but to be evoked, of everything good, pure, great and noble. He entered with all his heart into the hopes and fears, the troubles and aspirations of youth; and I have the sad conviction, that among the thousands who will miss his kindly presence and manners, none will more acutely feel the loss than the troops of boys and girls whom he used always in his own happy, genial way to style 'his children.' I have but few more words to add. If in some respects he, whom a dread disaster has snatched from us in the prime of his bodily and mental vigour, reminds us of that Hobab who knew our encampment in the wilderness and was to us in the place of eyes, there was one feature in his character in which he recalls the example of the best of men and the most faithful of God's servants. 'The man Moses was exceedingly meek.' Seldom could those words be more truly applied than to one whose name I will not mention here, whose name in life was ever mentioned least where his work was greatest. He was in truth one of those rare beings whose chief happiness was in seeing and making others happy, whose greatest pride it is to see and make their people honoured. For us, his brethren in Israel, whom he will no longer accompany in the journey of life, there is nothing left but to bewail the burning which the Lord hath kindled. The congregation were deeply affected during the sermon.

One of the last acts of Mr. Michael Henry before the lamentable accident which caused his death was a deed of kindness to a Stepney Boy, as the following letter will testify :—

Tuesday evening, June 15, 1875.

Dear Mr. Payne,—If * * * has not yet a situation, tell him to call on Messrs. * * * * between 10 and 12 o'clock in the forenoon and mention my name. Let him say he is a Stepney boy.

Yours, &c.,   M. HENRY.

⁎ From all sides expressions of condolence and profound sympathy for the late editor of this journal reach our office. The geniality of his manners, his urbanity and kind-heartedness are especially dwelled upon by such of our correspondents as had either come into personal contact with him or had been befriended by him. It affords a melancholy satisfaction to the staff of this journal to see how much beloved and how highly respected its chief was.

"Jewish World," June 25, 1875.

When the history of the Anglo-Jewish community of modern times receives the attention of the historian, no man should occupy a higher position amongst the illustrious individuals who have shed lustre on our escutcheon than the late Michael Henry. On the roll of true benefactors his name should stand foremost as one who loved his fellow men with an engrossing affection which found its vent in deeds of brotherly kindness. All his worldly possessions were ever at the disposal of the necessitous ; his heart always yearned for the poor and suffering, and his generous hand followed the promptings of that noble heart. Simple and unaffected was the way in which he dispensed his charity ; it was natural that he should be good, and he appeared to be unwilling to receive thanks or praise for the benevolence he practised. He wished for no public acknowledgment of his bounty; he was satisfied to keep in the rear and watch the effect of his liberality; he might have passed away in obscurity had not his brethren opened their eyes to the nature of the man. He is dead! The hand that gave a kindly pressure to the poorest and humblest, is cold and still; the beaming countenance from which the rays of benevolence shone, is placid and immoveable; the heart which beat for the poor and lowly has ceased its pulsations; the busy brain throbs not again. Michael Henry is no more! It was but a few days since that we saw him strong and happy; full of health and vigour, and overflowing with that kindly humour which endeared him to all; we saw him amongst the children he loved so well, and who loved him as a father. He was happy then in the consciousness of his good work having achieved success. May he be happy now in those realms where all is light and love and beauty!

It will be long before the community will realise the great loss which it has sustained. At the present moment we can hardly think that the noble-minded gentleman lies under the cold sod bereft of all sense and activity. But a few days ago his intellects were clear and bright, his laugh happy and almost boyish in its unaffected merriment, his almost feminine heart brimful of tenderness and sympathy. The talents which he undoubtedly

possessed were always at the command of the community
whose interests he guarded with jealous care, and when
he wrote, it was never to hurt, never to wound or offend
—ever to heal, conciliate, and bring into closer friendship Jew with Jew. Nothing was too humble for him
to do ; nothing too great for his achievement ; he entertained no contempt for that which was small and
insignificant, and was not daunted by that which appeared
high and unattainable. To a kind and affectionate
disposition he united a strength of purpose and manly
resolution which gained him the admiration of all with
whom he came into contact. He was not rich in the
world's goods, but to all he had the poor were welcome.
He was a messenger sent from Heaven to do naught
but good to human creatures, and to teach them that
we have more to live for than the aggrandisement of
self and the accumulation of wealth ; he came to show
us that man was created to love his fellow man, to be
merciful, generous, patient, and God-fearing. He was
a jewel lent by God to sparkle and illumine his surround-
ings ; the Almighty has reclaimed His loan, and may
that jewel now cast its effulgence around its heavenly
setting ! He is gone, and we mourn his loss. Can it
be possible that the great mind is closed for ever, and
that the loving heart beats no more ? Will little children
not once again sit upon his knee, and pour their prattle
into his willing ear ? Will the poor never more wait upon

his steps, and load their blessings upon his unwilling self? Shall we then not more behold him gallantly assisting in rolling along the burden of our nation? Alas, Michael Henry is dead, and we can but bedew the earth that covers him with our tears, and send forth our lamentations to the Most High! He is dead! May his soul rest in peace!

May the love and devotion to the cause of our people and humanity recommend him to that just God who knows the movements of every heart, the thoughts of every mind, the comings-in and the comings-out of all the creatures He has placed upon earth. May our Heavenly Father teach us to respect the memory of our lamented brother by a strict adherence to the righteous path in which he walked, and the pious ends to which he devoted his life. Let us hope that God has taken him to Himself, and that the bright spirit of Michael Henry dwells with Him he served so well.

Michael Henry, who met with his death in the fearful manner already made known to the public, was but in his 46th year, being born on Feb. 19, 1830, at Eltham House, Kennington. He was the youngest son of Abraham Henry, of Ramsgate, and afterwards of London. At an early age he exhibited unmistakeable signs of talent; for at the City of London School—where he, in common with many other now well-known co-religionists, received his education, under Dr. Mortimer, who always took great pride in his Jewish pupils—he gained numerous distinctions, one being a classical prize in the fifth class. He imbibed his taste for literature from his mother, Emma Henry, a daughter of the Rev. S. Lyon, of Cambridge, a lady of many accomplishments, whose volume of poems, published in the year 1812, was the first printed work of an English lady of the Jewish community. Her gentleness and kind disposition greatly influenced Mr. Henry in after life, and he often confessed to the writer of these lines that to his mother he owed many of his acquirements. While still young, Mr. Henry was appointed sub-editor of the *Mechanics' Magazine*, the first cheap scientific journal, of which the late Mr. Clinton Robertson, one of the compilers of the "Percy Anecdotes," was editor. Mr. Henry's contributions to that magazine were very valuable and much appreciated by the public; and his articles in the *Mining Journal* and other periodicals of a similar nature gained him considerable celebrity in scientific circles. He also edited the *Inventors' Almanack*, which appeared for a number of consecutive years, and wrote an elaborate defence of the Patent Law, which he dedicated to the late Lord Westbury. Those who remember the old days of the *Weekly Dispatch* will probably not have forgotten Michael Henry's stirring war song, "Go forth, thou Gallant Fleet," which appeared in that journal during the year 1856. He was also the author of a letter on

the " Registration of Trade Marks," which appeared in
the *Journal of the Society of Arts,* and which led to the
Government taking action in the matter. Eventually,
through the publication of this letter, a Registration of
Trade Marks Committee was formed in the House of
Commons, and a bill proposed in Parliament, but not
passed. In 1869, on the retirement of Dr. Benisch
through illness, Mr. Henry was appointed Editor of the
Jewish Chronicle, a post he held up to the time of his
death. Thus it will be seen that our friend Michael
Henry was a man of varied attainments, his knowledge
embracing a wide area of subjects. He had not lightly
skimmed the surface of things; he was no superficial
thinker, but had dipped deeply into the well of knowledge, and had taken deep draughts of its contents. If
one did not always agree with what he wrote, one had
the satisfaction of knowing that his utterances were be-
gotten of impartiality and fairness. His conversation
was always worth listening to ; a vigorous speaker, without being strikingly original, he never failed to arouse
the strictest attention ; and when from earnest and
sober language he lapsed into wit and humour, he could
not but succeed in exciting the greatest merriment
amongst his listeners. There was nothing pedantic
about Michael Henry, nothing flimsy or unreal ; he was
a downright honest man, blunt and emphatic in his
utterances, eager and desirous to praise when necessary.

But he was seldom—we may say never—known to have
visited with censure or contempt the deeds of any fellow
creature; he took a favourable view of human weak-
nesses, and gazed upon our frailties as the outcome of a
nature we cannot control. He was, nevertheless, very
sensible of dishonesty and meanness. His was an en-
thusiastic character, lifting him above the convention-
ality of these practical days; he was moved by a kind
of idealism which made him view humanity with benevolent eyes, and see in the peccadilloes of his fellow men
but very small blemishes, for which their erratic nature
was responsible. It may be said that he had not a
single enemy in the world; those who knew him well
and had discerned his character could not but love him.
He was free and open, and while not courting attraction,
he laid his heart open for inspection by the style in
which he conducted the business of his life—helping the
distressed, aiding the rich in their arduous endeavours
to help the poor, and exerting himself only in behalf of
others. We indulge in no fulsome adulation when we
say that seldom has his like appeared on earth; few,
unfortunately very few indeed have been the men who
on the earth were not earthly, as was Michael Henry.
There was no sacrifice he would not make to benefit his
people; nothing he would not strive to do in order to
enhance the community of which he was so brilliant an
ornament. He never waited to be asked to engage in

work calculated to effect some desirable result; he originated, designed, canvassed, corresponded, and laboured with his busy brain till the venture on which he had set his mind was safely launched. Then his gentle nature and sensitive soul would shrink from the public acknowledgment of his achievement, and he would be joyfully content to retire behind the scenes, watch the spectators applaud the episodes in the drama of which he was the anonymous creator, and express a delight—which we know was sincere and heartfelt—when others were accredited with the work which he had accomplished by dint of great exertion. Those who dived deeply into the innermost heart of hearts of Michael Henry often marvelled at his wonderful modesty, his dislike of praise, and indifference to any kind of public recognition of his virtues. In some men this indifference to celebrity would have discouraged a desire to benefit humanity; but with the noble gentleman we have lost for ever it was different. He loved "to do good by stealth, and blushed to find it fame !"

Looking at Mr. Henry's labours on behalf of the Jewish community we are struck with the indefatigable energy he imported into his unceasing work. To every undertaking, no matter its character, so long as it was intended thereby to benefit somebody, he lent his valuable aid, and set about the performance of his self imposed duties as if his life depended upon the exacti-

tude of their accomplishment. There are men in every
sphere who will, at the outset of any enterprise, readily
assume a responsible position in connection with it;
should the venture not be so successful as was antici-
pated by its sanguine projectors, they tire of it, and
arrive at the conclusion that there can be no possible
utility in maintaining what they have commenced, especially as they derive no personal profit from the
concern. Michael Henry displayed characteristics, in
the course of his honourable career, diametrically
opposed to the principles of such men; failure never
filled him with dismay, and though endowed with a by
no means inconsiderable amount of sensitiveness, which
reached almost to nervousness, he fought valiantly
against the tide of adversity, well knowing that in the
end every good cause must surely gain. Without wish-
ing to deprive any gentlemen of the credit due to their
exertions, we may observe that the Stepney Jewish
School will be a lasting monument of what one man can
do. It is very true that the success of that institution is
owing in a great degree to its competent officers and
managers, but it will be generally conceded that it would
never have attained to its present height of popularity
but for the ministrations of Mr. Henry, who, as honorary
secretary, a most frequent visitor, an able teacher and a
warm friend of the children, did more than the public
know to place the Stepney School in the position it now

occupies. Stepney School was indeed the favourite of the lamented gentleman, and we cannot without emotion think of the good natured simplicity with which he went about, what he called, his duties in connection with it. Very often did we see him trudging through the streets on a cold wintry day, defying alike snow and ice, purchasing baskets of fruit, cakes, and toys with which to delight the children at Stepney he loved so well. Indeed, one of his latest letters, which must have been written very shortly before the occurrence of the fearful accident which led to his death, was written in behalf of a " Stepney Boy," for whom he was anxious to obtain a situation—and which, we are informed, has proved successful. On his arrival at the school the pupils would shout for joy and cling to his garments as if he were their natural protector. Then would he sit down amongst them, pour out some pretty tale, or charm them with some kind advice. Their laughter is hushed now, and tears stand in the eyes of the boys and girls who were wont to welcome his presence. Michael Henry has left us, and the children have lost a dear, dear friend.

His distaste for publicity of any kind precluded the community, except those members of it most intimately connected with him, from gaining much insight into the nature of his communal work. It was Michael Henry who originated the foundation of the institution now

known as the United Synagogue, the desirability of the
establishment of which he set forth in a very able pamphlet ; and it is very certain that his suggestions became
the basis on which that now successful corporation was
founded. The Jews' College is another institution in
which Mr. Henry took a profound interest—an interest
which was demonstrated in a most substantial manner,
for he was not the man to give anything the benefit of
his name without the advantage of his personal and
pecuniary aid. The General Benevolent Society, a very
excellent charity, was almost wholly managed by him,
and its members—both Jews and Christians, and those
who, without distinction of creed, benefited by its existence—will often bless the memory of that kind gentleman, who was honoured and beloved by all. The
Hebrew Literature Society was another of his pet ideas,
and we believe that he first broached the idea of its
establishment. If that society has not achieved the
success which we expected would fall to its share, it was
not owing to any lack of exertion on the part of the
deceased.

In giving this lengthy notice of the late Michael
Henry we do not think that any apology is due to our
readers. As an earnest worker in behalf of the community, as the friend of all who desired his help, as a
scholar and a gentleman, his memory has claims upon
our esteem which cannot be disregarded. Had Michael

Henry been a rich man there would have been, so to speak, no limit to his philanthropy ; as it was his generosity was limited only by his means. From the sympathy which has been everywhere evinced for the bereaved, and the universality of the sorrow felt at his loss, it is evident that the community is not unmindful of the nobility of Michael Henry's character, and that his deeds will be commemorated in some lasting manner is our earnest wish. We have great benefactors amongst us, always ready to promote charitable undertakings— men whose hearts and purses are always open to the poor; but it is to be doubted whether there exists in the whole of our nation a man of the like of Michael Henry.

The funeral took place on Monday last. Intimation had been forwarded to all the metropolitan synagogues of the time appointed, and it was requested that friends of the deceased would meet at the cemetery at about 11 o'clock. This arrangement was generally observed, and a very large number of persons made their way by train to Willesden Junction, which is within half-an-hour's walking distance of the cemetery. The *cortége*, which consisted of thirteen mourning coaches, and many private carriages, left Argyle Square at 10 o'clock, and arrived at the cemetery shortly after 11. A detachment of boys of the Stepney Schools (who wore crape on their hats and arms) to the number of sixty, was stationed at either side of the pathway leading to the hall ; they, together with their head master, Mr. W. Ash Payne, their former master, Mr. E. H. Valentine, and others of the teaching staff, had been conveyed by private omnibuses, and had specially passed the residence of the deceased, out of respect to his valued memory. Some of these youths are now filling situations provided for them by the exertions of Mr. Henry. In another part of the ground was to be met, under the charge or their Principal, the Rev. John Chapman, a detachment of pupils of the Jews' Hospital, one of whom carried a banner draped in mourning. Following the mourning coaches which conveyed the relatives and more intimate friends of the deceased and the clergy, was that specially engaged for the students and the Principal of Jews' College (Dr. Friedlander)—a private omnibus, with twenty-five pupils and the teaching staff, having proceeded direct from the college to the cemetery.

The carriage way leading to the hall was lined with spectators anxious to take part in the melancholy proceedings of the day. When the carriages had discharged their occupants the hall was densely filled. The assemblage, numbering between 300 and 400, was thoroughly representative, comprising as it did members of every metropolitan congregation. A deputation from the Anglo-Jewish Association was also in attendance. As for the clergy, it is no exaggeration to say that on no previous occasion have they assembled in such numbers,

and it would have been a matter of difficulty to distinguish who was absent.   Poor as well as rich testified by
their presence the esteem in which they held the departed.

Before the commencement of the funeral service,
wreaths and immortelles were placed on the coffin, round
which were stationed six former and six present pupils
of the Stepney Schools.   This was followed by the
reading of the service by the Rev. A. L. Green, who was
so overcome with emotion, that it was with great difficulty
he was enabled to proceed.   The scene at this moment
was painful and solemn in the extreme, for scores of
grown-up men, and numerous children of various schools
in which Mr. Henry took such profound interest, could be
seen shedding tears, while grief was plainly expressed on
the countenances of many who suppressed such mani-
festations.   The procession, headed by the coffin—the
bier on which it was rested being carried by the above
referred to Stepney boys—then proceeded slowly to the
grave into which the coffin was lowered, flowers and
wreaths of immortelles being strewed on the lid.   The
remainder of the service having been performed in the
hall, the assemblage dispersed, groups of persons being
met with in all directions discussing the merits and
virtues of the lamented gentleman.

———

At the Bayswater Synagogue, on Sabbath last, the
Rev. Dr. Hermann Adler preached on the tragic theme

which filled his hearers' and his own heart. He took as his text the words of Isaiah lvii. 1, 2, "The righteous perisheth and no man layeth it to heart: and merciful men are taken away, none considering that the righteous is taken away from the evil to come. He shall enter into peace; they shall rest upon their couch each one walking in his uprightness." He showed how these words solved in some measure the mystery of the early death of the righteous. Who can tell if our loved and lost one had been spared, what trials might have been in reserve for him, what sins and temptations might have overtaken him, what sorrow and suffering might have fallen to his lot? How much better is a brief life with its bright and hallowed memories than a prolonged existence with its many possible evils? He has entered into peace, no more to be claimed like a slave to the oar of toil. He has been gathered in to his fathers, he has been invited to the dear ones who have gone to their rest, he has entered the communion of the great and good of all ages. And he walks in righteousness still. The memory of his deeds and worth is deathless and imperishable. If we recall all the good he has wrought, all the glowing words he has spoken, can we regard his as an early and untimely death? At the conclusion of his sermon the preacher, in addressing two Barmitzvah boys, quoted some remarkably appropriate words from a paper addressed to boys, contributed by Mr. Henry to the Sabbath Readings, which moved his hearers to tears.

The Rev. S. Singer, preached an affecting sermon at the Borough Synagogue, on Sabbath last. In the course of his remarks, the preacher, whose subject was the conversation between Moses and Hobab (Numb. x. 29–31) relative to the departure of the latter for his native land, referred to the sad disaster which had deprived the community of one of its best friends, who "knew our encampment in the wilderness and was to us in the place of eyes." He who had just departed for that land from which God had sent him to us, joined to the faculty of sympathising with his people the power of working for them. His talents were ever at the service of those who sought the good of their nation. His pen, "the pen of a ready writer," strove to effect the advancement of Israel and their elevation in the eyes of the nations of the earth. Yet was he, who spared himself so little, ever generous towards the faults of others. If he was to us in the place of eyes, it was mainly to detect whatever good there was in the community. He left to others the ungracious task of discovering all blots and blemishes from which the best of us were not free. In an age when every man deemed himself especially commissioned to become the critic and the censor of his neighbour, this genial friend of Israel filled a useful and important place.

D

But while all classes of the community found room in his affections, there was one section of it in particular to whose interests he seemed to address himself with an almost undivided energy. He had an inextinguishable faith in youth, a manly love for those who would one day themselves be men. None perhaps would feel his loss more acutely than the children into whose wants and aspirations he knew how to enter with all the ardour and devotion of his genial nature. In one respect he might be said to recall the example of the great teacher of our race. Rarely could the praise of modesty and meekness be more justly assigned than to him, whose name there was no need to mention in that holy house, whose name in life was ever mentioned least where his work was greatest. His brethren of the house of Israel might well set themselves now to bewail the burning which the Lord had kindled; but, in the midst of the bereavement by which they were bowed down, they might derive their truest consolation from the glorious promise to which they had that day listened, " Thus saith the Lord, if thou wilt walk in my ways and observe my charge, if thou wilt also judge my house and keep my courts I will give thee a place among them that stand here."

The sad occurrence also formed the subject of a sermon preached by the Rev. A. L. Green, at the Central Synagogue, on Sabbath last.

JEWS' COLLEGE.

10, FINSBURY SQUARE,
LONDON, E.C., JULY 7, 1875.

DEAR SIR,

The Council of Jews' College, at a meeting held on the 4th inst., resolved unanimously to tender to you, and your esteemed family, the assurance of their sincere condolence and profound sympathy on the sad loss you have sustained in the lamented death of Mr. Michael Henry.

The Council have to deplore the loss of one of its most esteemed members, who, by the constant and parental interest which he took in all that was connected with the institution, had endeared himself alike to the Council, to the officers, and to the students and pupils.

The Council most earnestly pray that God may grant you comfort and solace in your trouble, that acquiescence in the Divine will may strengthen you to bear your affliction, that the many virtues of your lamented brother may be a copious source of consolation to you, and that you may be spared for many years in uninterrupted health and happiness.

The accompanying resolutions were unanimously adopted by the Council.

Believe me, dear Sir,
Yours very faithfully,
N. ADLER, DR.,
President.

Richard Henry, Esq.

RESOLUTIONS.

" 1.—That this Council deeply deplores the irrepar-
" able loss which the Community has sustained in the
" demise of Michael Henry, who, by his sterling qualities
" of heart and mind, as well as by his energetic exertions
" to promote the religious, moral, social, and intellec-
" tual welfare of his brethren, had earned the highest
" regard of all classes.

" 2.—That this Council greatly laments the loss of
" their colleague, who, during a great number of years
" had been one of the most zealous workers on behalf
" of this institution, who contributed so largely to its
" success, and who had, by his loving care and advice,
" endeared himself to its students and pupils.

" 3.—That a copy of these resolutions, together with
" a letter of condolence, be forwarded to the family of
" Mr. Henry, and that the resolutions be advertised in
" the Jewish press.

" N. ADLER, DR.,

" July 4th, 1875." "*President.*

SHEFFIELD HEBREW CONGREGATION.

Copy of resolutions passed at a meeting of the
members of the Hebrew Congregation, on Sunday, July
11, 1875.

" 1.—That this Meeting begs to express its profound
" sorrow at the untimely death of Mr. Michael Henry,

" its former representative at the Board of Deputies.

" 2.—That this meeting begs to place on record its
" recognition of the invaluable aid rendered on all occa-
" sions by Mr. Henry to this congregation through his
" excellent advice and advocacy, and which contributed
" so largely to the establishment of the synagogue and
" school in Sheffield.

" 3.—That this meeting offers its sincere condolence
" and sympathy to the family and friends of the deceased,
" who have the melancholy satisfaction of knowing that
" their grief is shared in common by the whole body
" of Jews.

" 4.—That a subscription list be opened to assist in
" carrying out the memorial in contemplation to the
" revered memory of the deceased, with the view of
" giving effect to the objects so dear to his heart.

" 5.—That a copy of these resolutions be forwarded
" to the family of the deceased, and advertised in the
" Jewish press."

FREE LECTURES TO JEWISH WORKING MEN
AND THEIR FAMILIES.

At a meeting of the Committee of the above Association, it was unanimously resolved :—

" 1 That this committee deeply deplores the irrepar-
" able loss the community has sustained in the lamented

"demise of their colleague Mr. Michael Henry, who was
"one of the originators of the movement for providing
"Free Lectures to Jewish Working Men and their
"Families, and to the success of which he so largely
"contributed by his earnest advocacy and his personal
"co-operation.

"2. That this Committee, to the various members of
"which Mr. Michael Henry had endeared himself, by
"his unceasing efforts to promote the moral, social and
"intellectual advancement of our nation, as well by his
"amiability of character, desires to express to all those
"nearly related to him, its deepest sympathy in their
"bereavement, and to offer them that condolence which
"emanates from the most affectionate regard for the
"departed, and from the knowledge of the severe loss
"the Association has, in common with the whole com-
"munity, sustained by his death.

"3. That a copy of these resolutions be forwarded to
"the family of Mr. Michael Henry, and that the same
"be advertised in the *Jewish Chronicle* and *Jewish World.*

"(Signed)   A. L. GREEN,
"*Chairman.*

"LAWRENCE SAMUEL,
"*Hon. Sec.*

"LONDON, 29th JUNE, 1875."

GENERAL BENEVOLENT ASSOCIATION.

15, BERNERS STREET, OXFORD STREET, W.,

JUNE 29, 1875.

DEAR SIR,

I am directed by the Committee of the General Benevolent Association to transmit to you the enclosed resolutions passed at a special meeting which was held yesterday, together with the letter of condolence to which the second resolution refers.

The engrossed copy will be prepared and forwarded as soon as possible.

I am, dear Sir,

Yours truly,

HENRY J. KISCH,

R. L. Henry, Esq.   *Hon. Sec. pro tem.*

————

At a special meeting of the Committee of the General Benevolent Association, held on the 28th June, 1875, at the house of the Chairman, Mr. J. N. Lindo, the following resolutions were unanimously passed :—

" 1. This meeting desires to record its sense of the " loss the General Benevolent Association has sustained " by the melancholy death of its founder and honorary " secretary, Mr. Michael Henry, to whose able and " zealous labours ever since the foundation of the Asso- " ciation—a period of 27 years—the success of the " charity is mainly due.

" 2. The Committee of the General Benevolent
" Association being desirous of expressing their sincere
" sympathy with the members of the family of their
" lamented honorary secretary on the occasion of his
" sad and sudden death, resolve to send a letter of con-
" dolence to them, and that the same be engrossed on
" vellum and suitably framed."

J. N. LINDO,

Chairman of the Committee.

LONDON, 28TH JUNE, 1875.

The Committee of the General Benevolent Association cannot find words in which adequately to describe
their sense of the irreparable loss they and the Association have sustained by the sad and sudden death of their
much loved and lamented honorary secretary, Mr.
Michael Henry.

The Committee feel that in losing him they have lost
their chief member, who, since he founded the Association in 1848, has been its principal worker and moving
spirit, who with devotion of time and attention, and at
the sacrifice of all personal considerations, performed for
the long course of 27 years the onerous duties of honorary
secretary—duties which, performed in his conscientious
and tender-hearted manner, involved continual unofficial
private disbursements—incessantly exerting himself to
promote the object of the Association which was ever

dear to him, the aid of those requiring temporary assistance so as to effect their permanent benefit, striving
always to extend its sphere of usefulness, and to save
its funds at his own cost from outlay for working
expenses. He cheerfully continued to fulfil the duties
of honorary secretary year after year, notwithstanding
the increase of various other calls upon his time and
purse.

The Committee beg to express to the family of their
deeply-lamented colleague the profoundest sympathy
with them in their bereavement. The Committee trust
that the universal love, esteem, and respect entertained
and manifested for the departed, may afford some consolation to his family in their affliction.

WILLIAM J. LITTLE, M.D., *President.*

JULIAN GOLDSMID, M.P.,	ALFRED LONGSDON,
J. W. BATTLEY,	F. D. MOCATTA,
HENRY BESSEMER,	NATL. MONTEFIORE,
J. M. JOHNSON,	JOSEPH SEBAG,
Vice-Presidents.	*Vice-Presidents.*
J. N. LINDO,	ALBERT KISCH,
Chairman of Committee.	*Deputy Chairman.*
W. H. BERLINDINA,	R. F. HARE,
R. BRIGHAM,	ALFRED HENRY,
ISAAC N. CARVALHO,	CHARLES JOHNSON,
L. M. FINZI,	EDMUND JOHNSON,
J. AUSTIN GARRARD,	E. M. LITTLE,
H. J. GASKILL,	DAVID LONGSDON,
MICHAEL A. GREEN,	HENRY LUMLEY.

HENRY J. KISCH, *Hon. Secretary (pro tem.)*

STEPNEY JEWISH SCHOOLS.

LONDON, JUNE, 1875.

DEAR SIR,

At a meeting of the Committee of the Stepney Jewish Schools, held on the 20th inst., it was unanimously resolved to offer you and your esteemed relatives, on the part of the Committee, the expression of our deep and heartfelt sympathy on the irreparable loss you have sustained in the death of that noble-minded, tender, and true-hearted man, whom you had the good fortune to call your brother.

Associated as we have been with him for so many years, we have had ample opportunities to appreciate his unflagging zeal, his utter abnegation of self, and his truly religious fervour; and it is not too much to say that all of us—his colleagues on this Committee—feel that in him we have lost a brother. No words of ours can lighten the blow that has fallen on the relatives to whom he was so devoted, but it must surely be a source of some consolation to them to know that their grief is shared and felt as a personal loss, not only by the pupils of the Stepney School who have lost in him a second father, but by every member of the community to whose service he gave the best part of his life, the best efforts of his ever active and energetic mind.

We pray that the Almighty may spare you from further trials for many years, and that you may have the satisfaction of witnessing the realization, both in his family and in the community, of the wishes which were dearest to your lamented brother's heart.

We remain, dear Sir,

Yours faithfully,

MARCUS N. ADLER, *President.*	ISAAC A. JOSEPH.
M. H. BENJAMINS, *Vice-President.*	HENRY LUMLEY.
JOSEPH MIERS, *Treasurer.*	DERMIT CASTILLO.
LIONEL L. ALEXANDER. *Hon. Sec. (pro. tem.)*	J. BERGTHEIL.
MOSES JOSEPH.	HENRY KISCH.
M. S. WALEY.	WOLF MYERS.
H. MONTAGU, *Hon. Sec.*	HENRY HYMANS.
MORRIS JOSEPH.	MICHAEL A. GREEN.

JEWISH SCHOLARS' LIFE BOAT FUND.

DEAR SIR,

As representatives of the Jewish Scholars of the United Kingdom, and of the Jewish Scholars' Life Boat Fund, we beg to express to you and your family the sincere grief and sorrow that is felt by the Jewish Scholars of the United Kingdom on the sad bereavement you have sustained through the demise of your late lamented brother, Mr. Michael Henry. We, who feel his loss as a friend, beg to offer you our heartfelt sympathy.

Michael Henry, the true friend of the scholars, has departed. We are at a loss to know what to write, so inadequately can words convey the feelings of the multitude of lads who congregated on Wednesday last at Jews' College, to honour the memory of the man who, for them, had performed wonders! The following resolutions were passed: —

" 1. That we (the honorary secretaries of the Life " Boat Fund) write to you as senior member of the " family, expressing the deep regret and sorrow, love " and respect, which was felt by the Jewish Scholars, and " sympathising with you in your loss.

" 2. That, as a testimonial of the great regard which " was felt for the founder of the movement, as well as in " every Jewish philanthropic cause, the Life Boat to be " purchased be called the ' Michael Henry.' "

We would that you had been there, in order that you might yourself have seen the grief-stricken countenances of these boys who have lost their best friend.

Again, dear friends, accept our sympathetic condolence in this great trial, and may God Almighty grant you consolation.

ת׳׳נ׳׳צ׳׳ב׳׳ה׳׳

We have the honour to be, dear Sir,

Your most obedient servants,

JOSEPH LAMBERT,

MORRIS J. SAMUEL,

Joint Hon. Secs. Life Boat Fund,

6, Delamere Crescent, Bayswater.

Richd. L. Henry, Esq.

JEWISH ASSOCIATION FOR THE DIFFUSION OF
RELIGIOUS KNOWLEDGE.

60, OLD BROAD STREET,
LONDON, JULY 7, 1875.

DEAR SIR,

I am desired to transmit to you the following resolutions unanimously passed by the General Committee of the above association :—

" That this Committee deeply lament the loss " sustained by the demise of their esteemed colleague, " Mr. Michael Henry, whose kind and energetic exer- " tions, and most valuable intellectual labours, on behalf " of this Association, rendered inestimable services to " this institution and the community at large.

" That this Committee desire to express and hereby " tender to the bereaved family of the late lamented " Michael Henry, their deepest sympathy and very sin- " cere condolence for the irreparable loss sustained of " one who, by his benevolence and long continued " public services, had justly gained the love and esteem " of every member of the community.

" That a copy of these resolutions be forwarded to " the family of Mr. Michael Henry, and that the same " be advertised in the Jewish newspapers."

I am, dear Sir,
Faithfully yours,
SYDNEY M. SAMUEL,
Hon. Sec.

Richard L. Henry, Esq.

UNITED SYNAGOGUE.

BOROUGH NEW SYNAGOGUE CHAMBERS,
HEYGATE STREET, WALWORTH, S.E.,
29TH JUNE, 5635, 1875.

DEAR SIR,

I am instructed to inform you that at a meeting of the Committee of the Borough New Synagogue, held yesterday, the following resolution was unanimously passed.

" That this Committee begs to offer to the family of " the late Mr. Michael Henry their most sincere and " heartfelt condolences, on the sad loss they have " recently sustained."

I have the honour to be,
Dear Sir,
Yours very faithfully,
S. SINGER, *Secretary.*

STEPNEY JEWISH SCHOOL CHILDREN.

STEPNEY JEWISH SCHOOLS,
71, STEPNEY GREEN.

DEAR SIR,

We scarcely know what to say to you by way of sympathy in the great sorrow which has overtaken you, except that we share the loss equally with you, for if you have lost a loving brother, have not we, as it were, lost a devoted parent? one who was never weary of doing good to the children of the Stepney Schools.

Let this, then, be our prayer on this solemn and sorrowful occasion : that we may each one of us strive to live in the light of the bright example which he has bequeathed to us, so that we may become upright and conscientious men and women, and thus realize the prayer that he has so often prayed for us.

May the God of Consolation be very near to you, and grant you a happy issue out of all your afflictions.

(Signed)

E. NORDON,	L. JACOBS,
C. SHMITH,	S. FRIEDEBERG,
D. SASSERATH,	A. ISAACS,
B. MOSS,	J. MOSS,
I. ROSE,	J. DE MEZA
C. DAVIDS,	N. DE MEZA,
L. MYERS,	A. VALENTINE,
D. RICARDO,	S. SASSERATH,
H. ABRAHAMS,	D. DAVIS,
H. TOURNOFF,	P. HARRIS,
A. JACOBS,	I. SOLOMONS,
L. MYERS,	J. STERN,

On behalf of the Boys' School.

JANE NORDEN,	EMMA MOSS,
LIZZIE VAN CREWELL,	CELIA MOSS,
ROSA DURAN,	LENA COHEN,
BETSY VALENTINE,	JANE SEAFIELD,
JULIA VALENTINE,	ANNE ABRAHAMS,
REBECCA NORDON,	MATILDA MARKS,
ESTHER WOOLF,	ANNIE WACKS,
CATHERINE LEVENE,	HARRIET VOLACK.

On behalf of the Girls' School.

"JEWISH CHRONICLE" COMPOSITORS.

"JEWISH CHRONICLE" OFFICE,

43, FINSBURY SQUARE, LONDON, E.C.

MR. HENRY.   JUNE 23, 1875.

SIR,

We, the compositors employed at the *Jewish Chronicle* office, beg to express to you and, through you, to the other members of your family, our heartfelt regret at the sad fatality which resulted in the death of our much respected editor and friend, Mr. Michael Henry.

During the period in which he filled the post of editor he ever endeared himself to us by his extreme kindness, urbanity and friendly disposition toward us. We assure you that his loss is acutely felt by us all, and his death has created a void in our midst which it will be difficult to fill up.

Trusting that the Almighty will grant you strength to bear the heavy blow He has inflicted on you and on the entire community, and that he may console you in your affliction, we beg to remain

Your obedients servants,

THOMAS A. WINTER.   GODFREY JOSEPH.

ABRAHAM DE WILDE.   ABRAHAM WOOLF.

HENRY WINTER.   ALBERT CANNAR.

EXTRACTS FROM LETTERS OF CONDOLENCE.

From Dr. B. ARTOM, Chief Rabbi of the Spanish and Portuguese congregations :—" I grieve for him, but " also for his family and the community. Pray, let me " know the time of the funeral, as I wish to pay a last " tribute of regard to the departed. May God give you " consolation."

From LIONEL L. COHEN, Esq. :—" I will not now " enlarge how deeply we feel with you on the loss we " have all sustained. It is too great to need descrip- " tion, and too recent to offer condolence."

From JACOB A. FRANKLIN, Esq. :—" My own special " experience enables me to appreciate his labours for " the communal welfare at a cost little understood by " those whose best interests he has been privileged to " advance. I was reminded by a warmhearted letter " from him, on occasion of the recent Pentecost, how " kind had been his consideration for my earlier " strivings for the same sacred cause as his feeble " pioneer. I little thought when he recently called to

E

"cheer me after my attack of illness that he would be
"summoned hence before me. His yearning was, in
"his own words, for 'rest.' Be consoled by conviction
"that he has gone to his 'reward.'"

———

From THOMAS SMITH, Esq.:—"The brief tribute
"paid to your late lamented brother in the *Chronicle*
"received yesterday, even with my limited acquaintance,
"I can fully endorse, and feel assured that in addition
"to the sad loss to your family circle, it is also a public
"calamity to a vast concourse of your race."

———

From JOHN G. JACOB, Esq.:—"Death must come
"to us all, but to some more painful than others; so, I
"fear, must have been the case of Mr. Michael Henry.
"From all I hear and know, 'he has lived respected,'
"and 'died lamented.' May we all leave as good a
"name behind us."

———

From MARCUS N. ADLER, Esq.:—"I have just
"learned that the funeral of your lamented brother
"will take place on Monday morning.
"   "Permit me thus far to intrude upon the sacredness
"of your grief to enquire whether the family would

"permit say twelve of the Stepney School boys to carry
"the remains of one whom they so loved to their last
"resting place.

"The school looked upon him as their father just as
"he regarded them as his children, and of course they
"will all be at Willesden to pay him their last token of
"respect.

"But a few days ago, after that happy gathering at
"Stepney, he wrote to me, 'as to myself I am in the
"seventh heaven of delight.' He is there now in truth."

———

From JOSEPH SEBAG, Esq. :—"Although only one of
"a very numerous body of his admirers and well-wishers,
"no one had a greater appreciation of his excellent
"qualities. In fact I have never met with so good and
"pure minded a person, nor one who so willingly and
"intelligently devoted his time and energies for the
"good of others, and, I believe, but too often forgetful
"of himself."

———

From P. SAMUEL, Esq. :—"I can hardly realise that
"those eyes of his which sparkled with a lustre rarely
"seen in mortal men are now closed for ever. I can never
"forget the pleasant evening I passed with him in your
"house when his inestimable mother was alive. He has

" withered in all the flower of his spring. A life
" uniting business and literature so well is not often
" seen, and it is difficult to understand that providence
" which removes men who can be so ill spared from
" this world of inferior natures."

From A. LINDO-HENRY, Esq.:—" I am also glad that
" the Stepney distribution was over, as I think of all
" things a successful Stepney prize giving was one to
" give him the greatest possible pleasure. While that
" school lives his memory must live, for who can forget
" the time and labour he has spent on that institution?"

From ESTHER DE COSTA:—" I cannot express to
" you the shock and regret I felt when in the *Times* of
" Friday I read the sad and fearful death of your
" lamented kind and talented brother; not only will his
" family mourn his loss, but the Jewish community, for
" he devoted so much of his time and abilities for the
" benefit of his co-religionists, that his early demise is a
" national loss. It is sad to think that one in the prime
" of health, strength and usefulness should be removed
" from among us; but we may be sure that his good
" deeds and kind heart have obtained for him everlasting

" happiness in the next world, and a permanent memo-
" rial in this, which in time to come will be a consolation
" to the bereaved ones that now mourn his loss."

———

From ALEX. PRINCE, Patent Agent (to Mrs. R. L.
Henry) :—" I beg to express our deep sympathy with the
" suddenly sad loss of Mr. Henry's brother, of which I
" was only this day informed at the Government Patent
" Office. I read the melancholy account in the papers,
" but was not aware it was your relative."

———

From SIR MOSES MONTEFIORE, Bart. (to Mr. Lewis
Emanuel) :—" I have been deeply grieved and shocked
" by the sad intelligence of the death of our lamented
" friend Michael Henry, and the terrible accident which
" occasioned it. I feel deeply for his relatives in so
" distressing a bereavement, and their sorrow is shared
" by the entire community, who deplore the loss of one
" of its chief ornaments. I should feel glad if you could
" take an opportunity of making known to the family how
" warmly I sympathise with them, and how sincerely I
" lament the death of our esteemed friend."

———

From WM. BLACK (to his brother):—"I felt very much "when I read about Michael Henry. I know nothing "but what appeared in the papers; but I do know that "a kinder, more unassuming, and, so far as I can judge, "a more talented man in his own profession hardly "existed. I am sure, from my very little acquaintance "with him, that his friends who knew him intimately "must mourn his loss very deeply."

The Members of the Sheffield Hebrew Congregation held a meeting on Sunday last, at which resolutions were passed expressing sorrow at the death of Mr. Michael Henry (who was formerly representative of the congregation at the Board of Deputies) and condolence with his family. It was also resolved to open a subscription to assist in carrying out the contemplated memorial. All our continental and American Jewish contemporaries contain biographical notices of the late Mr. Henry. The *Magid, Wochenschrift* and *Hebrew Leader* add some sympathetic comments on the benevolent career of the deceased. The *Jewish Record*, of Philadelphia, *Jewish Messenger* and *Hebrew Leader*, of New York, insert the announcements of his death between black borders.

"LONDON SUN," SEPTEMBER 5, 1874.

SOME EMINENT JEWS.

Mr. Michael Henry, the editor of the *Jewish Chronicle*, was born at Eltham House, Kennington, in 1830. He received his education at the City of London School, in which several now distinguished Jews underwent their scholastic training. Here he gained numerous distinctions, and at an early age exhibited a taste for literature. Mr. Henry is a son of the late Emma Henry, a gifted and accomplished writer, whose poems, published in 1814, comprised the first printed work issued by an English lady of the Jewish faith. These poems were well received by the newspapers of the period. Mr. Michael Henry in the earlier part of his life was the sub-editor of the *Mechanics' Magazine*, the first cheap scientific journal, of which the late Mr. Clinton Robertson, one of the compilers of the "Percy Anecdotes," was editor. Mr. Henry has also written some very valuable articles for the *Mining Journal*, and has contributed to several leading periodicals. He edited the *Inventors' Almanac*, and wrote a defence of the Patent Law, which he dedicated to the late Lord Westbury. He was also the author of the war song, "Go forth thou gallant fleet," which appeared in the *Weekly Dispatch* in 1856, and of the letter on the "Registration of Trade Marks," published in the *Journal of the Society of Arts*, and which led to the Government taking action in the matter. The ultimate result of Mr. Henry's letter was the formation of a Registration of Trade Marks Committee, and a bill proposed in Parliament, but not passed. Mr. Henry occupies numerous positions in the Jewish community, all of an honorary character. He is most genial and attractive in manner, and his largeness of heart has gained for him an extensive circle of friends and ad-mirers. As the editor of the *Jewish Chronicle* he is naturally possessed of great influence, and, indeed, Mr. Henry is one of the most popular and best-beloved Jews in London. He is a bachelor, but his love for his fellow creatures is not in the least diminished by that fact. The *Jewish Chronicle* has now been estab-lished over thirty years, and has always been noted for its respectability. It is well written, and its articles vie with the compositions of many general papers. But it must be confessed that its enunciations are somewhat one-sided, all matters relating to the Jews being chroni-cled from the most favourable point of view. From a perusal of its pages it might be imagined that Israelites were, for the most part, a body of immaculate individuals, not burdened with the iniquities of the rest of living creatures. On questions of Jewish communal import, the *Chronicle* does not state its opinions altogether im-.partially, and those affairs which do not conduce to the credit of the Jews, it ignores altogether. This is no fault of Mr. Henry, who, personally, is one of the most independent and fair-play-loving men alive. The proprietors of that journal, however, are men of importance in the community, and as such have certain notions to which they are desirous of giving publicity. On the whole, the *Jewish Chronicle* is an excellent periodical, and much of the success it has attained is due in no small degree to the talents of Mr. Michael Henry, its able and respected conductor.

"JEWISH WORLD," OCTOBER 1, 1875, IN REVIEW OF YEAR 5635.

In June last, Michael Henry, after fearful suffering caused by an accident, breathed his last, and the Jews of England were plunged in mourning. The great good man, with his large honest heart brimming over with the milk of human kindness, is gone! Who will take his place remains to be seen.

"JEWISH CHRONICLE," JULY 9, 1875.

The echo of our laments over the death of the late Michael Henry is beginning to reach our shores. The first resounded in the *Archives Israelites*. Mr. Alexandre

F

Weill, in the July number, gives a brief biographical sketch of the deceased, characterising him as gentle and affable, having no enemies, but, above all, as most conscientious in the fulfilment of his duties. Several of the Berlin daily papers and the Amsterdam Jewish journals have also published biographical notices of the late Mr. Henry.

———

"JEWISH WORLD," MARCH 19, 1875.

———

We sincerely regret that Mr. Michael Henry has been compelled, through pressure of private business, to resign the post of Honorary Secretary of the Stepney Jewish Schools. The Committee of this institution can ill-afford to lose the services of a gentleman whose exertions have vastly assisted in the promotion of education among the Jews in the East-end of London. Mr. Henry has been more than a mere honorary official; he has been the life and soul of the schools, and has displayed an interest in their welfare altogether unprecedented in the careers of honorary secretaries. With all due deference to the successor of Mr. Henry, we venture to predict that it will be many years before we "look upon his like again." Not a master has been engaged in the schools, and not a pupil has ever crossed their threshhold, but who is ready to testify to the invariable kindness and courtesy with which he discharged the duties of his office. His pleasant and genial manner has endeared him to all classes of society; and Mr. Henry to-day enjoys the very enviable distinction of being one of the best beloved men in the Anglo-Jewish community. We trust, for the sake of the Stepney Jewish Schools, that he will not entirely withdraw himself from participation in the work of the institution. True, the impetus which he has given to the schools will cause them to flourish, still we should be sorry to see the captain retire from the vessel now that it is steered safely into port.

www.ingramcontent.com/pod-product-compliance
Lightning Source LLC
Chambersburg PA
CBHW022010050726
47499CB00008BA/3065